TEENAGE MUTANT NINJA TURTLES

EPIC TURTLE TALES

Random House 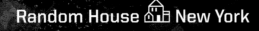 New York

©2015 Viacom International Inc. and Viacom Overseas Holdings C.V. All rights reserved. Published in the United States by Random House Children's Books, a division of Penguin Random House LLC, 1745 Broadway, New York, NY 10019, and in Canada by Random House of Canada, a division of Penguin Random House Ltd., Toronto. The stories in this work were originally published separately in different form as follows: *Saved by the Shell!*, in 2012; *Monkey Business*, in 2013; *Ooze Control!*, in 2013; *Red Alert!*, in 2015; and *Robot Rampage!*, in 2013. Pictureback, Random House, and the Random House colophon are registered trademarks of Penguin Random House LLC. Nickelodeon, Teenage Mutant Ninja Turtles, and all related titles, logos, and characters are trademarks of Viacom International Inc. and Viacom Overseas Holdings C.V. Based on characters created by Peter Laird and Kevin Eastman. ISBN 978-0-553-52471-0
randomhousekids.com
MANUFACTURED IN SINGAPORE
10 9 8 7 6 5 4 3 2 1

CONTENTS

For fifteen years, four turtle brothers lived beneath the streets of New York City. In a secret lair in the sewers, Splinter, their martial arts teacher, trained them to be ninjas.

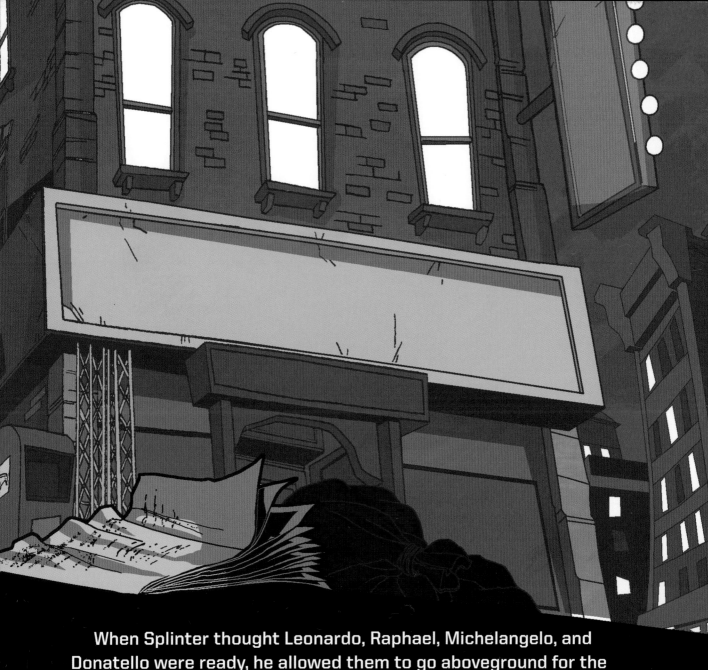

When Splinter thought Leonardo, Raphael, Michelangelo, and Donatello were ready, he allowed them to go aboveground for the first time.

New York City was dark and dirty—and the Turtles loved it!

The city was filled with incredible surprises. The best one was . . . pizza!

"I never thought I'd taste anything better than worms and algae," said Raphael. "This is amazing!"

"It's great up here," said Michelangelo.

4

As the Turtles headed back to the sewer, they saw a girl walking with her dad. Her name was April.

"She's the most beautiful girl I've ever seen," Donatello said.

"She's the *only* girl you've ever seen," Raphael replied.

Suddenly, a van screeched to a stop. Strangers jumped out and grabbed April and her dad. The Turtles rushed to help, but they kept bumping into each other. Leonardo hit Raphael. Michelangelo tripped over Donatello. While the Turtles were tangled up, the strangers escaped with April and her dad.

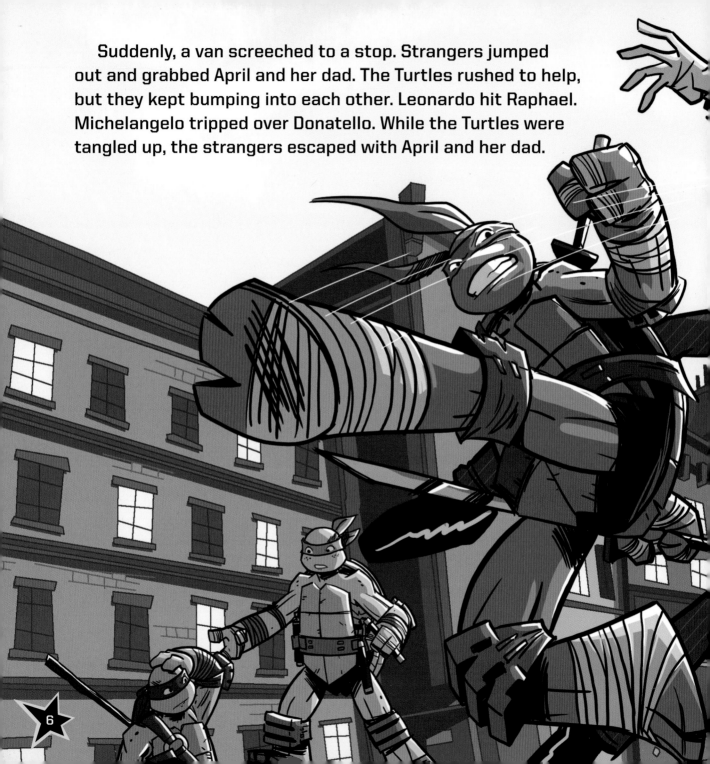

One bad guy was left behind. Michelangelo hit him with his *nunchucks.*

BLOOP!

A weird pink blob popped out of his chest. The bad guy was really a robot with a brain! The brain scurried away before Michelangelo could show anyone. His brothers didn't believe him.

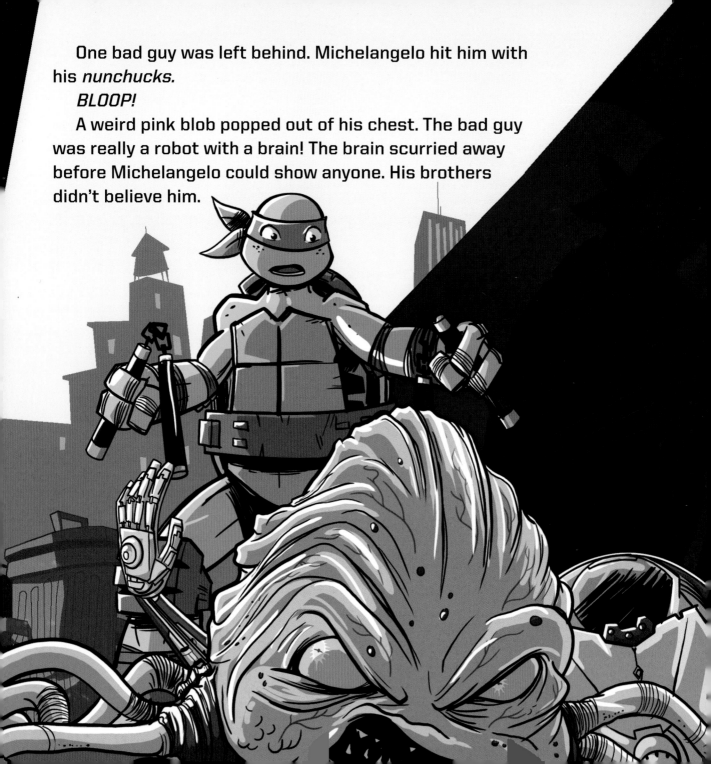

Back in the sewer, the Turtles told Splinter about the failed
rescue attempt.

"I need to train you as a team," Splinter said. "Next year you can
go to the surface again."

But Donatello couldn't wait. He wanted to save April right away.

Splinter nodded. "Then you will need a leader." He chose Leonardo.

The next night, the Turtles returned to the streets. They found the van. Raphael wanted to attack immediately, but Leonardo said they should be patient. They waited and watched. The van drove off, and the Turtles followed it . . . to the bad guys' hideout.

The Turtles snuck into the hideout. They discovered that Michelangelo was right—the bad guys really were brain-like aliens! The aliens were called the Kraang, and they wanted April's dad, who was a famous scientist, to help them with an evil plan.

Some Kraang forced April and her dad into a helicopter. As it took off, Donatello leaped onto one of its landing skids to stop them. The helicopter spun and rocked. April fell out.

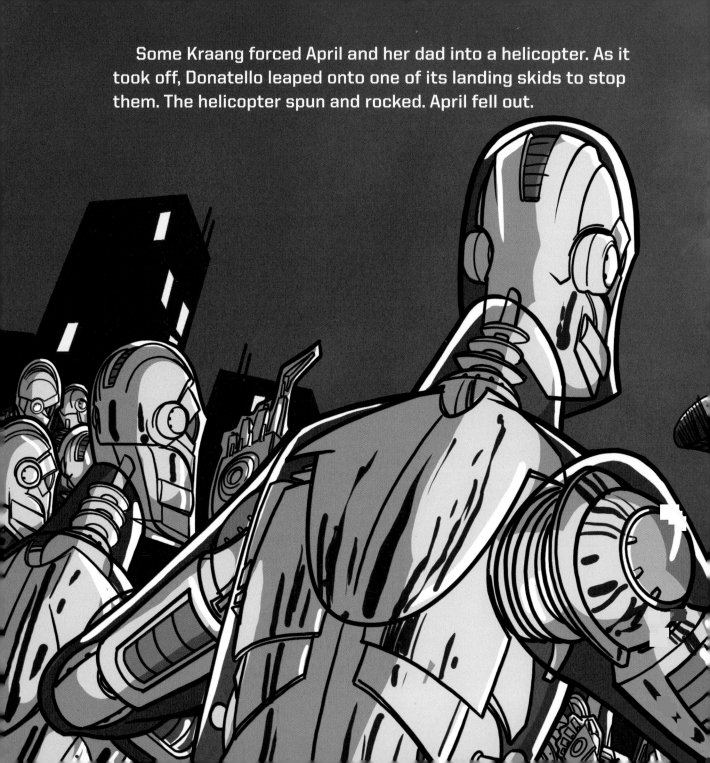

Donatello saved April, but the Kraang flew away with her dad.

"Looks like we'll have to fight our way out," said Leonardo.
"It's about time," growled Raphael. The Turtles sprang into
battle. They fought as a team, and they were unstoppable.

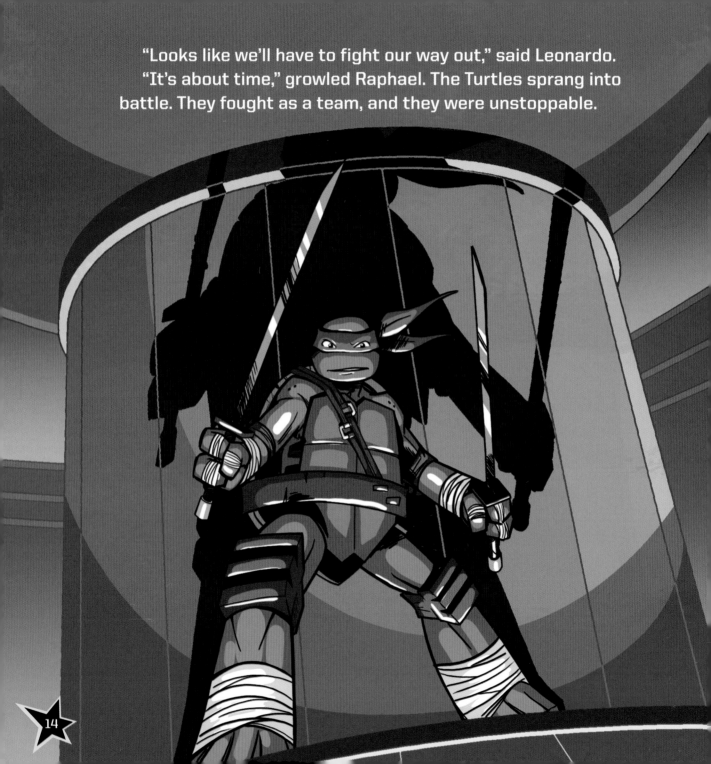

Suddenly, Leonardo had an idea. He ran to the hideout's power generator. The Kraang turned their blasters toward him and fired.

Leonardo jumped aside at the last second.

KABLAAM!

The generator exploded and destroyed the hideout as the Turtles and April tumbled away from the blast.

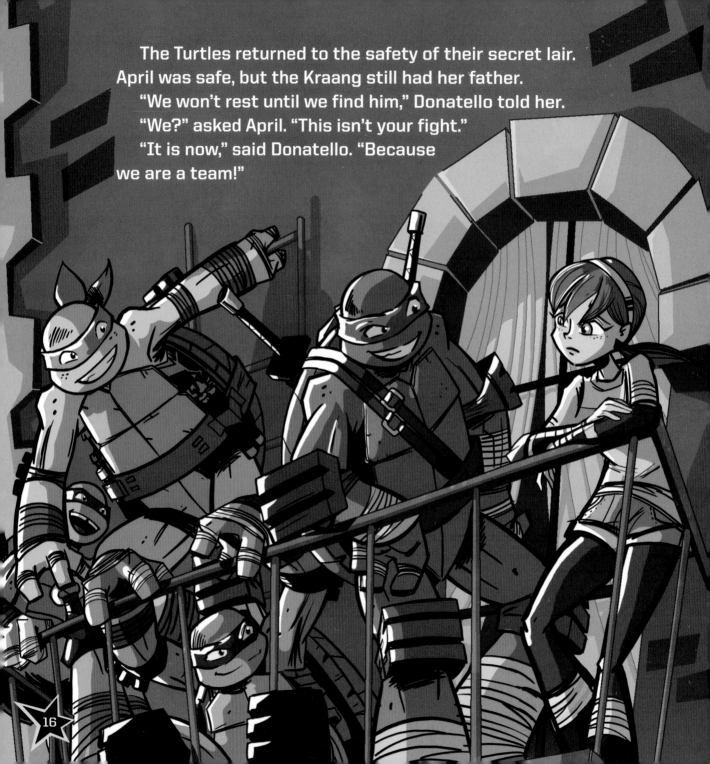

The Turtles returned to the safety of their secret lair.
April was safe, but the Kraang still had her father.
"We won't rest until we find him," Donatello told her.
"We?" asked April. "This isn't your fight."
"It is now," said Donatello. "Because
we are a team!"

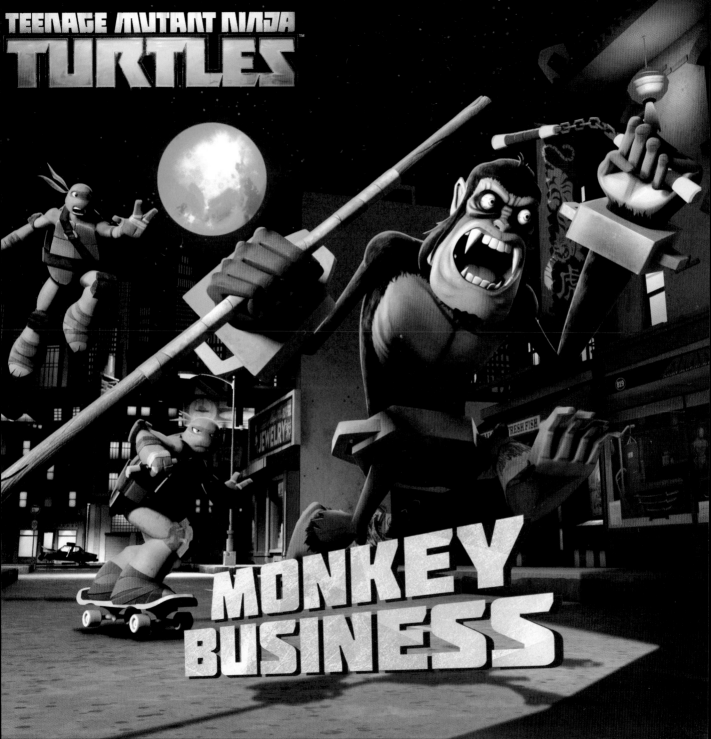

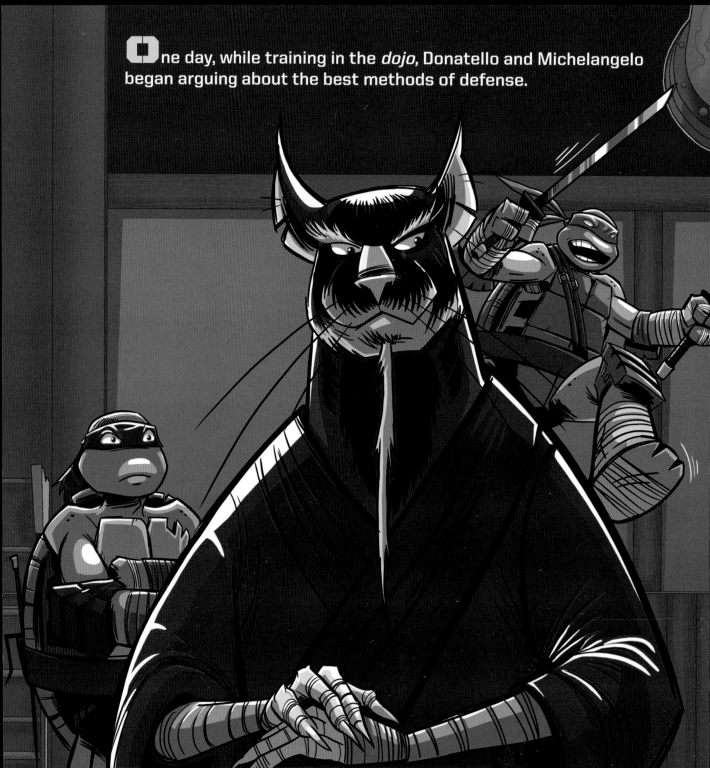

One day, while training in the *dojo*, Donatello and Michelangelo began arguing about the best methods of defense.

"Mikey, you need a plan for every attack," said Donatello. "Isn't that right, Splinter?"

"You must be fully in the moment so you can fight without thinking," replied Splinter.

Just then, the Turtles' friend April O'Neil ran into the *dojo*. "According to the news, a scientist named Tyler Rockwell is missing," she said. April's father, an important scientist, had been captured by an alien race called the Kraang. "Maybe the Kraang have taken this guy, too."

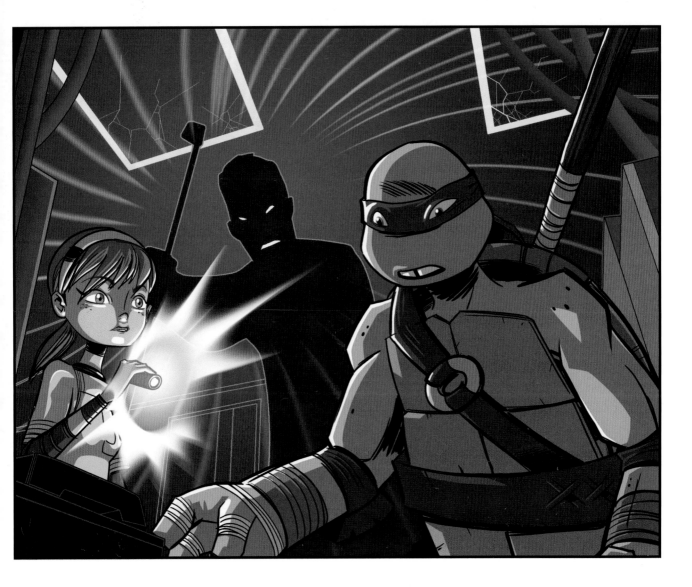

Donatello and April decided to investigate. They raced to Dr. Rockwell's abandoned lab. While searching the dark room, Donatello found a canister of mutagen—the mysterious Kraang chemical that had mutated the Turtles.

Suddenly, a shadowy figure attacked!

Donatello overcame the attacker. His name was Dr. Falco. He was the missing doctor's assistant. He revealed that Dr. Rockwell had been using the mutagen to perform strange experiments on a monkey.

"It looks like the monkey didn't like being locked up," Donatello said, investigating a mangled cage. He noticed a computer flash drive and slyly took it.

As Donatello and April left the lab, a giant monkey leaped from above!

"Watch out!" April yelled. "He's a dangerous mutant!"

"That makes two of us!" Donatello replied.

Donatello charged, swinging his *bo* staff, but the raging monkey knocked him back easily.

The monkey locked April in his massive arms, then paused.
They had a connection. April could read the monkey's mind, and
he could read hers. "Everything's okay," she whispered reassuringly.
The monkey relaxed, but then he ran away.

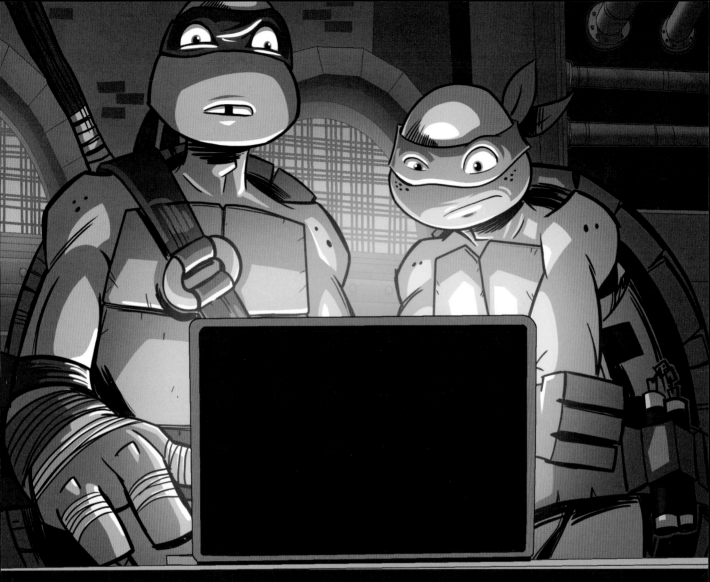

Back at the lair, Donatello analyzed the flash drive and learned that Dr. Rockwell was using the mutagen to give his lab animals psychic powers.

"That monkey can read minds!" Donatello exclaimed.

"Cool," Michelangelo said. "I wonder if he could tell me what I'm thinking—I've always wanted to know."

April and the Turtles went to find the monkey.

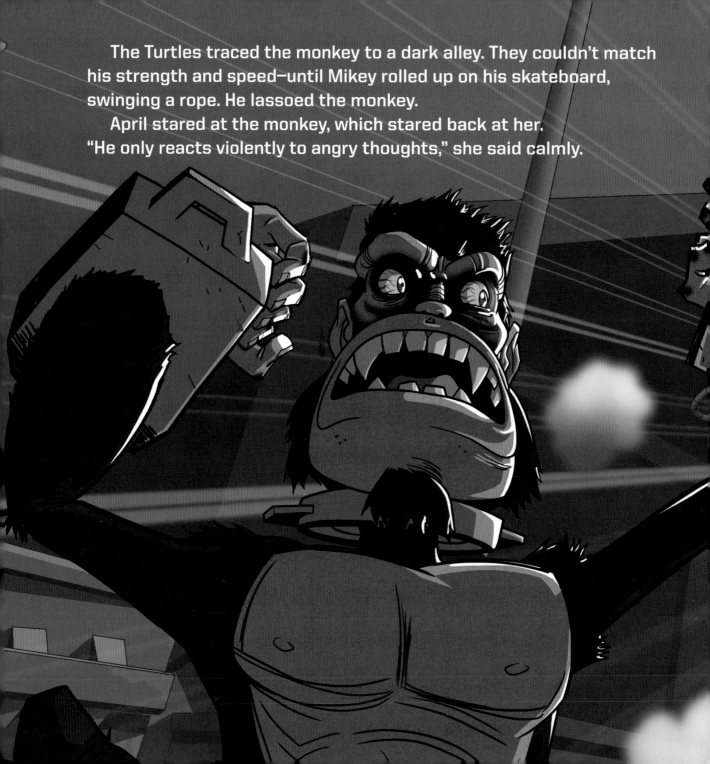

The Turtles traced the monkey to a dark alley. They couldn't match his strength and speed—until Mikey rolled up on his skateboard, swinging a rope. He lassoed the monkey.

April stared at the monkey, which stared back at her.

"He only reacts violently to angry thoughts," she said calmly.

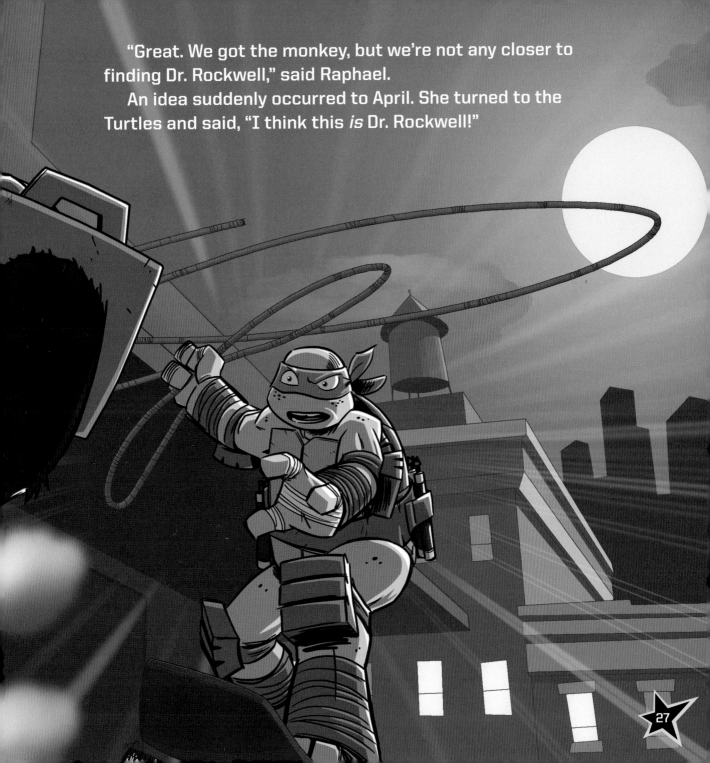

"Great. We got the monkey, but we're not any closer to finding Dr. Rockwell," said Raphael.

An idea suddenly occurred to April. She turned to the Turtles and said, "I think this *is* Dr. Rockwell!"

The Turtles returned the monkey to the lab, where they made another startling discovery: it was Dr. Falco who had used the mutagen on Dr. Rockwell!

"He was my guinea pig," Dr. Falco confessed.

"Well, it didn't work," Michelangelo said. "You turned him into a monkey!"

His *katana* swords flashing, Leonardo sprang at Dr. Falco.

The Turtles quickly realized that Dr. Falco had used the mutagen on himself, too—he could read the Turtles' minds! Knowing their attack plans before they struck, Dr. Falco was more than a match for the Turtles.

Suddenly, Donatello remembered Splinter's words: "You must be fully in the moment so you can fight without thinking." He cleared his mind and launched himself like a bolt of lightning. His flying kick hurled Dr. Falco across the room.

Dr. Falco realized he was defeated and quickly ran away.

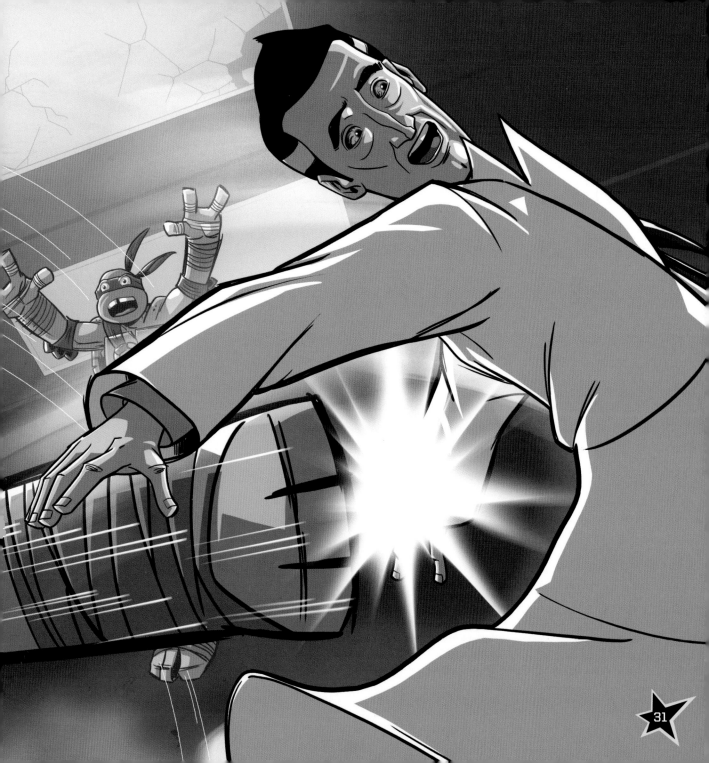

The Turtles knew they couldn't leave Dr. Rockwell tied up,
so they released him, and he bounded out a window.
They immediately heard a woman scream and a car crash.
"Um, maybe New York City isn't the best place for a psychic
monkey who reacts to angry thoughts," said Raphael.

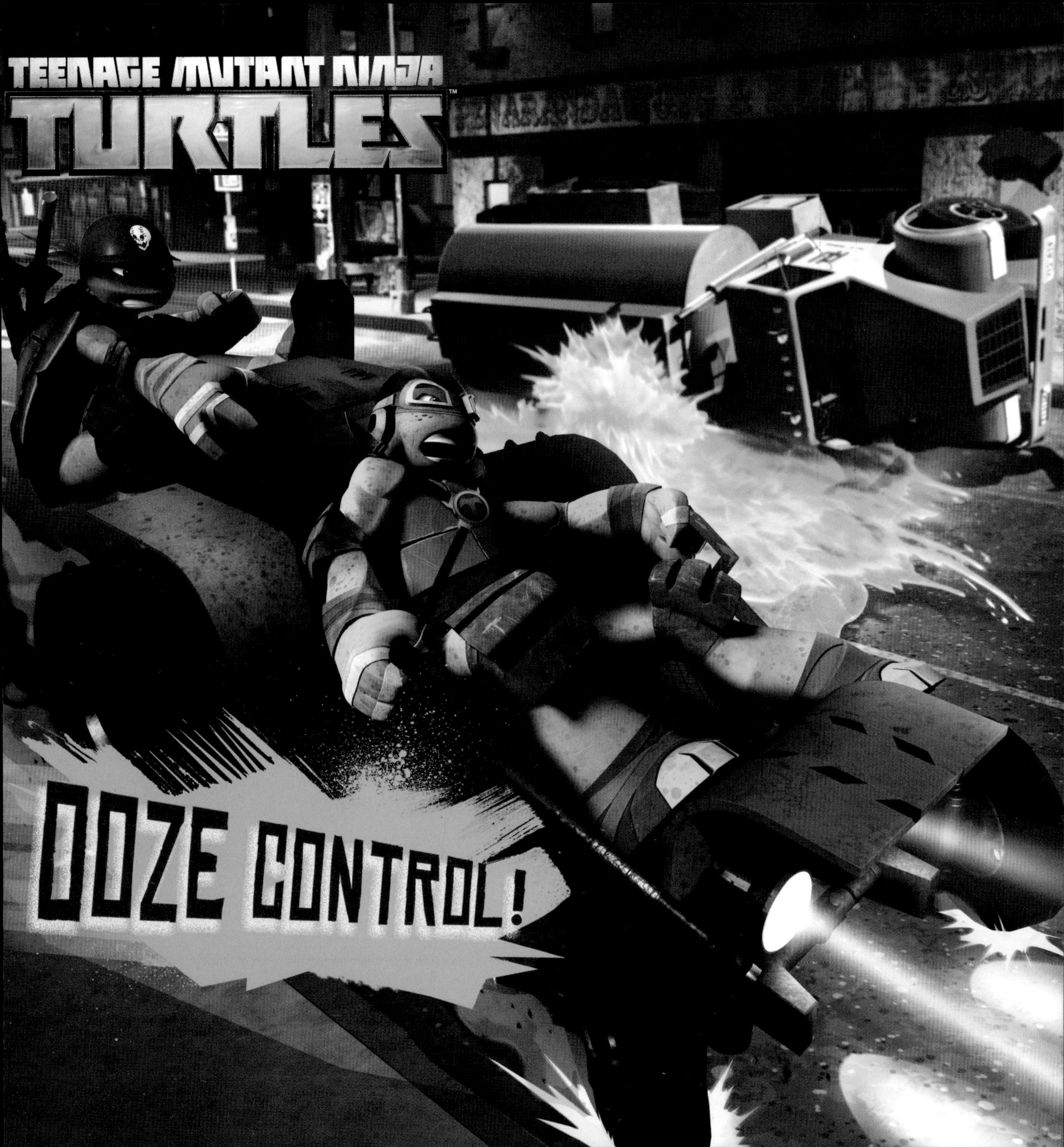
TEENAGE MUTANT NINJA
TURTLES™
OOZE CONTROL!

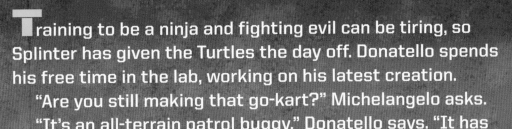

Training to be a ninja and fighting evil can be tiring, so Splinter has given the Turtles the day off. Donatello spends his free time in the lab, working on his latest creation.

"Are you still making that go-kart?" Michelangelo asks.

"It's an all-terrain patrol buggy," Donatello says. "It has detachable sidecars and—"

SPLASH!

Mikey hits Donatello with a water balloon.

"Dr. Prankenstein strikes again!" shouts Mikey.

Donatello chases Mikey, but he stops when he sees April O'Neil talking to Leonardo in the lounge.

She has made a terrible discovery—the evil Shredder knows that the Turtles live in the sewer. "He's going to destroy the entire sewer system to get you," she warns.

"We have to find out what his plan is," says Leonardo. "Let's go topside."

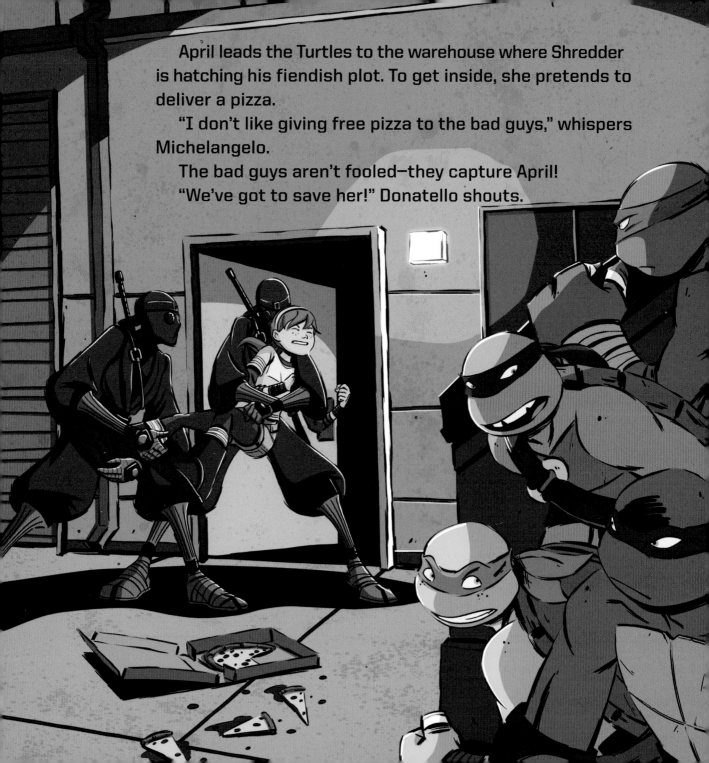

April leads the Turtles to the warehouse where Shredder is hatching his fiendish plot. To get inside, she pretends to deliver a pizza.

"I don't like giving free pizza to the bad guys," whispers Michelangelo.

The bad guys aren't fooled—they capture April!

"We've got to save her!" Donatello shouts.

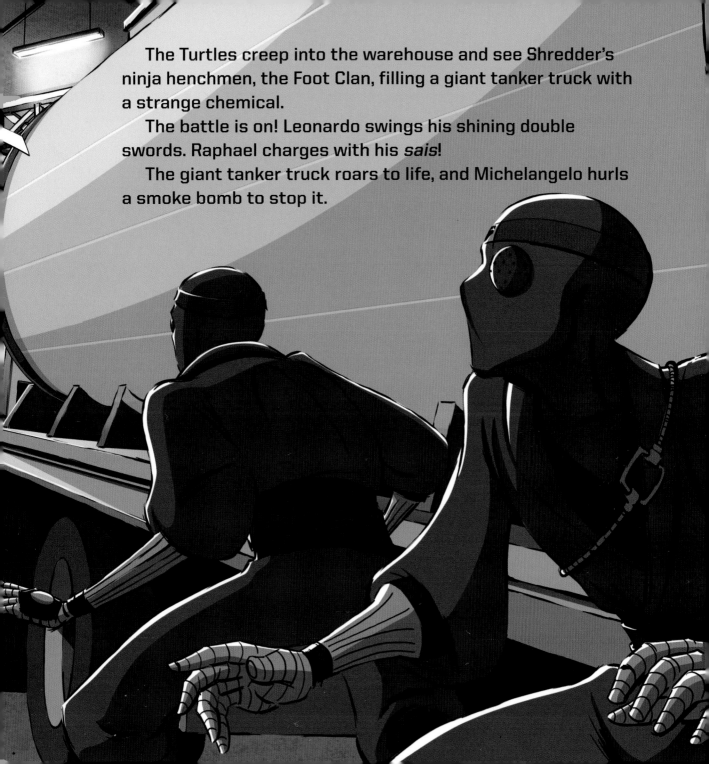

The Turtles creep into the warehouse and see Shredder's ninja henchmen, the Foot Clan, filling a giant tanker truck with a strange chemical.

The battle is on! Leonardo swings his shining double swords. Raphael charges with his *sais*!

The giant tanker truck roars to life, and Michelangelo hurls a smoke bomb to stop it.

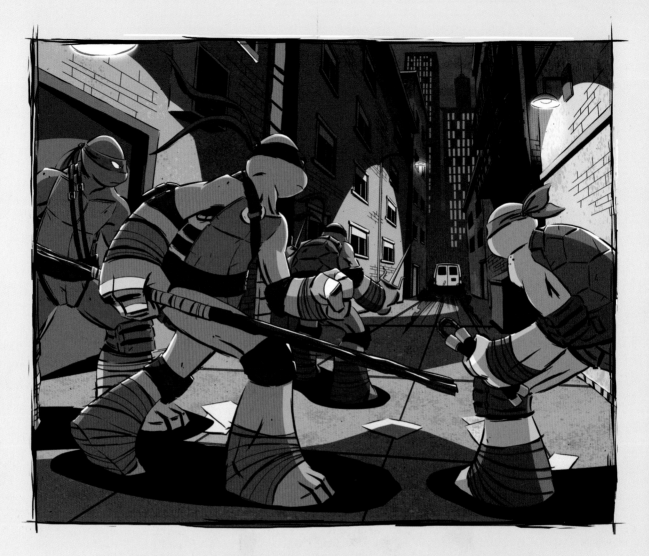

The Turtles can't stop the Foot Clan. April is driven away in a white van. The tanker thunders into the night.

"I figured out Shredder's plan," says Donnie. "That tanker is carrying a dangerous chemical. When mixed with water, it explodes. If it's poured into the sewer, everything will blow up—including our lair!"

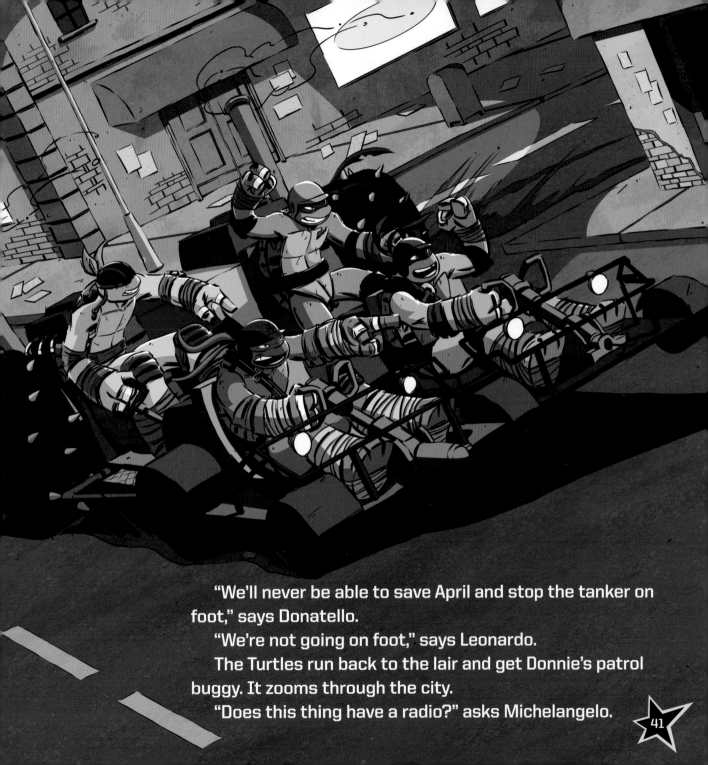

"We'll never be able to save April and stop the tanker on foot," says Donatello.

"We're not going on foot," says Leonardo.

The Turtles run back to the lair and get Donnie's patrol buggy. It zooms through the city.

"Does this thing have a radio?" asks Michelangelo.

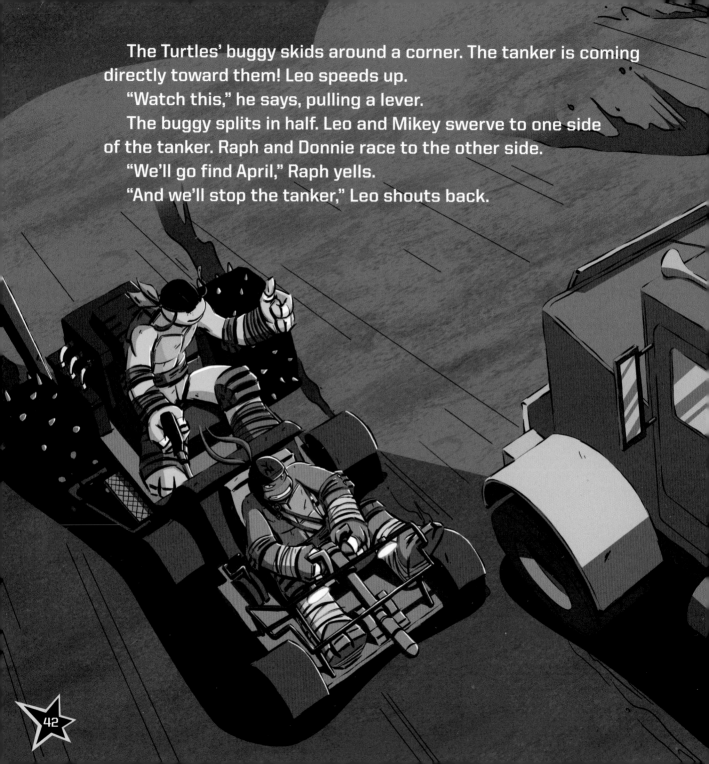

The Turtles' buggy skids around a corner. The tanker is coming directly toward them! Leo speeds up.

"Watch this," he says, pulling a lever.

The buggy splits in half. Leo and Mikey swerve to one side of the tanker. Raph and Donnie race to the other side.

"We'll go find April," Raph yells.

"And we'll stop the tanker," Leo shouts back.

Donnie and Raph find the van. Donnie hurls a throwing star and blows out a tire. The van skids to a stop. The two Turtles make quick work of the Foot Clan ninjas in a blaze of *ninjutsu*.

"Thanks," says April.

A few blocks away, Mikey and Leo find the tanker. The bad guys are carrying a hose from the tanker to an open manhole. They're going to pump the chemical into the sewer.

"We have to stop them!" Leonardo yells. "Do you have any water balloons, Mikey?"

Michelangelo smiles. "I sure do."

Leonardo leaps toward the tanker and slices open
its side with his sword. The chemical gushes out.
Michelangelo winds up and hurls a water balloon.
KABLAM!
The truck explodes as the two Turtles jump to safety.

The Turtles and April return to the lair to celebrate with pizza.

"This pizza smells kind of funky," says Donatello. "Where'd you get it, Mikey?"

"It's the one April dropped in the alley."

Everyone groans and throws their pizza back in the box—except Mikey.

"We live in a sewer," he says. "We can't be clean freaks! Oh well, more for me!"

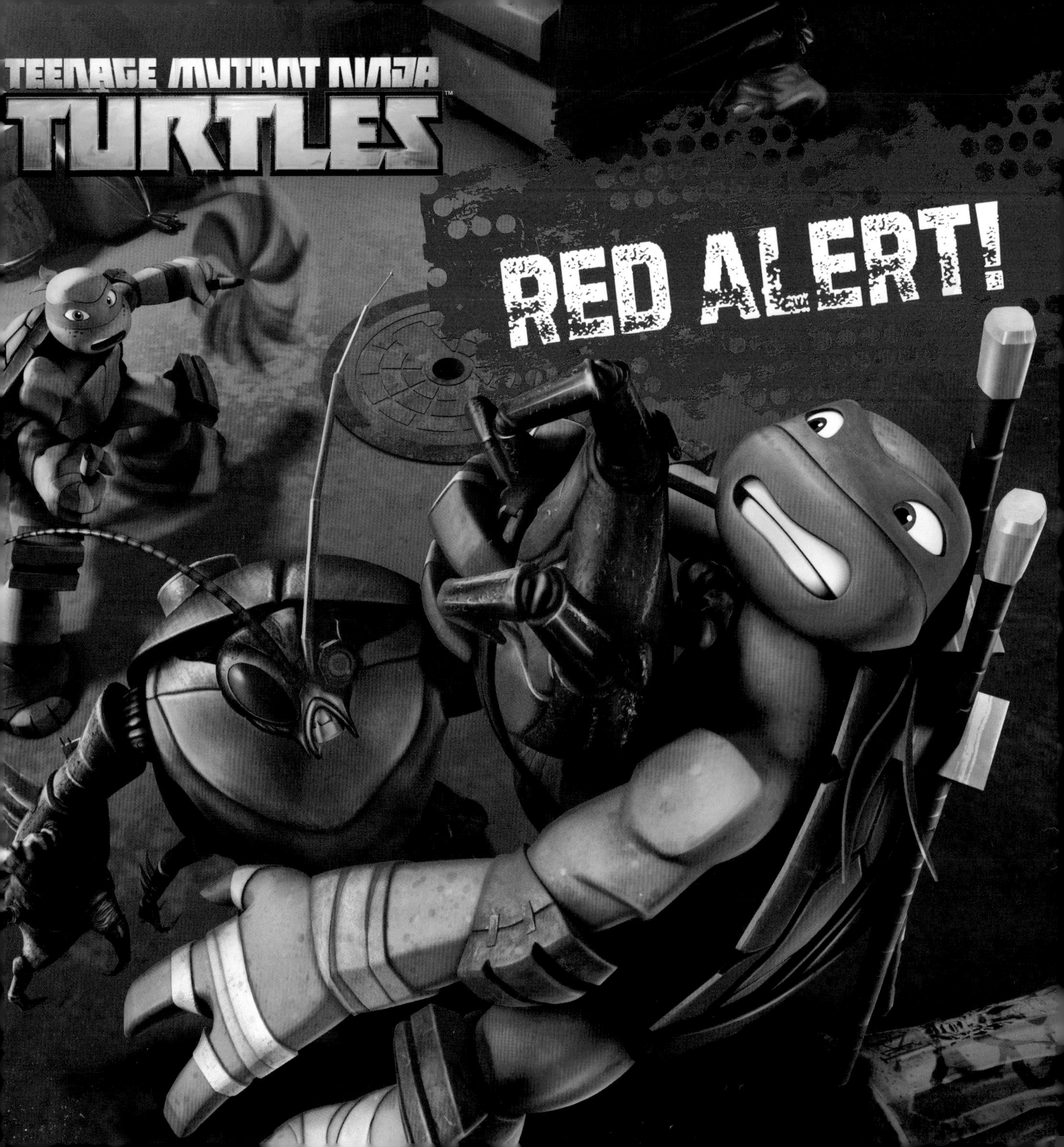
TEENAGE MUTANT NINJA TURTLES™
RED ALERT!

One evening, while the Turtles were eating dinner, a cockroach scurried across the table. Raph hated roaches. He shrieked, spilled his soup, and tried to squash the roach with his *sai*.

But this was no normal cockroach—Donnie had outfitted it with a camera and transmitters.

"We can spy on the Kraang with this cockroach," Donnie announced. "Whatever it sees, we can see."

"So we can watch Raph's freak-out again," Mikey said with a laugh. "Let's go to the replay."

That night, the cockroach spy snuck into the Kraang's secret headquarters. The Turtles watched its fuzzy transmissions from inside the *Shellraiser,* their armored assault van.

They overheard the Kraang's plan to drill to the center of the earth. All they needed was a diamond lens for their giant laser drill.

A hole that deep would flood the streets of New York with waves of lava!" Donnie exclaimed. "We've got to stop them."

He checked his maps of New York City. There was only one lab where the Kraang could get a diamond lens.

Suddenly, the cockroach's transmission stopped.

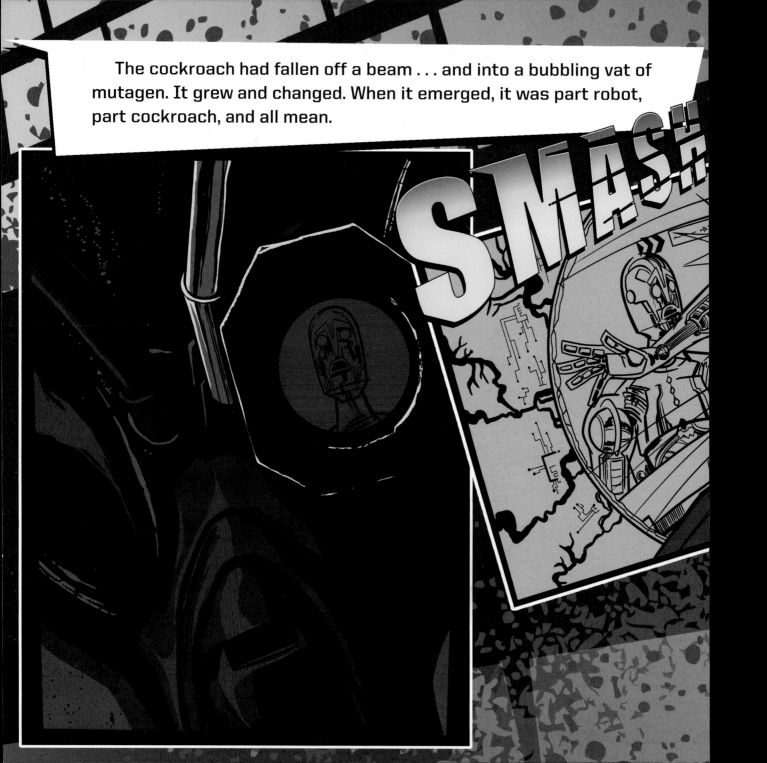

The cockroach had fallen off a beam . . . and into a bubbling vat of mutagen. It grew and changed. When it emerged, it was part robot, part cockroach, and all mean.

The giant roach marched through the lab, sighting Kraang-droids with its red robotic eye and destroying them with its giant claws and the spinning blade on its tail.

As the *Shellraiser* left for the lab, it hit something—the cockroach! Donnie recognized the camera and wiring. "That's our spy roach. He must have gotten into the mutagen!"

The Turtles charged the creature—except Raph. He was afraid to touch the slimy monster.

Instead, Raph stayed back and launched manhole covers. One hit the roach, knocking it out. The evil red eye went dark.

"Way to go, Raph!" the Turtles cheered. But when they looked back, the big bug was gone!

There was no time to look for it. They had to stop the Kraang.

The *Shellraiser* reached the lab just as two Kraang-droids were loading the diamond lens into a van. With *katanas* flashing, Leo led his brothers into battle. The Kraang fought back with their laser-pulse cannons.

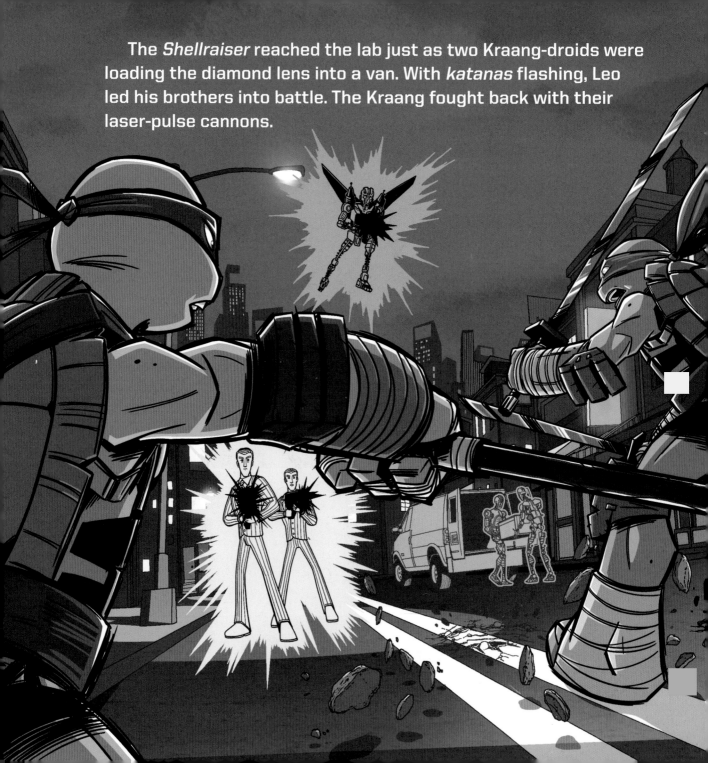

Then the giant cockroach stepped around a corner. It had followed the Turtles! Meanwhile, the Kraang escaped with the diamond lens.

Donnie's computer calculated that there was only one place the Kraang could drill into the earth's crust. The *Shellraiser* screeched away.

The *Shellraiser* raced to the Kraang compound, where the giant laser drill blazed away at the ground. Kraang guards stopped the Turtles at the gate—until Raph jumped over the wall on his Stealth Bike!

He had almost reached the drill when a slimy white creature swooped down from the sky. It was the cockroach, and it had shed its shell. It was bigger and grosser than ever—and it was hurling explosive eggs!

I'm not afraid of you!" Raph yelled, jumping from the bike onto the giant drill. "Come and get me!"

Raph wrestled the sticky creature, throwing powerful punches at it. When he had his chance, he dove for the lens and deflected the laser.

ZZZZ-BLAM!
The burning beam destroyed the cockroach and the giant drill.

"Raphael, you saved the city and conquered your fear of cockroaches!" Leo shouted. "Not bad for a Wednesday night."
The Turtles took off, leaving behind the smoldering remains of the laser drill . . . and one unexploded mutant roach egg.

One afternoon, April showed the Turtles a website she had made. "It's a message board where people can post strange things they see around the city," she explained.

Someone had posted a news video about a gas explosion in the warehouse district. April hit Pause. In the background they could see the Turtles' enemies, the Kraang—powerful, evil robots with blobby pink brains.

Since Splinter didn't want the Turtles to be seen in the daytime, April went to check out the warehouse on her own.

April spotted a Kraang-droid and followed it to a warehouse. She heard two robots talking strangely. "The mutagen will be tomorrow unleashing in the water supply," one said.

Mutagen was the radioactive ooze that had turned the Turtles into mutants. If the robots put it in the water, many people would mutate!

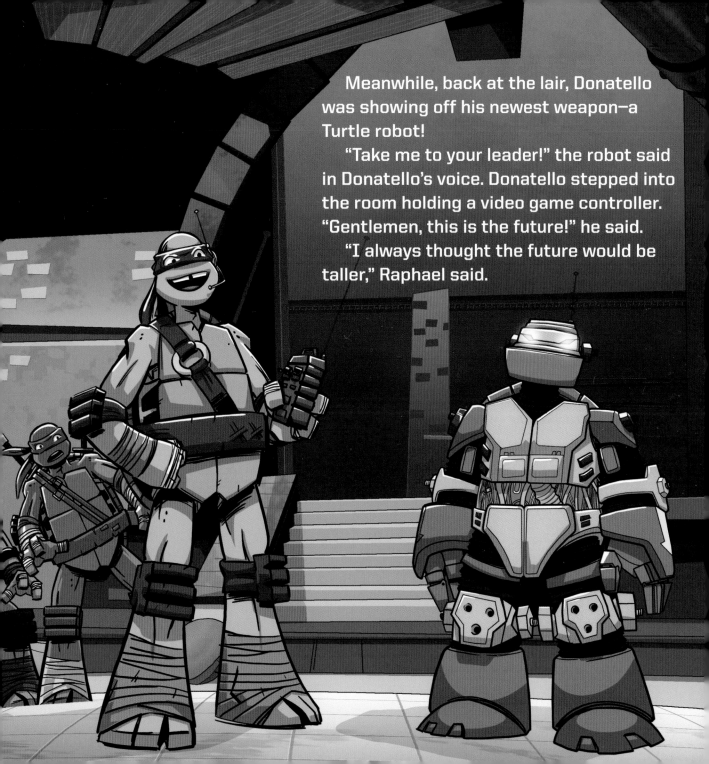

Meanwhile, back at the lair, Donatello was showing off his newest weapon—a Turtle robot!

"Take me to your leader!" the robot said in Donatello's voice. Donatello stepped into the room holding a video game controller. "Gentlemen, this is the future!" he said.

"I always thought the future would be taller," Raphael said.

"Isn't it cool?" Donatello said. "I built it from Kraang parts. It can do all the dangerous stuff while we stay safe."

"So it's for wimps," Raphael said.

"Try it," Donatello said. "Attack."

Raphael, Leonardo, and Michelangelo all sparred with the new robot. But none of their attacks could make a dent.

"Let's call it Metalhead!" said Michelangelo.

71

That night, Michelangelo, Raphael, and Leonardo went out into the city. They leaped across rooftops and waited on a ledge.

Clang! Clang! Clang! Metalhead slowly caught up with them.

Donatello was back in the lair, controlling the robot like a video game.

"Quiet!" Leonardo said. "Someone's coming!"

It was April. "We have to do something," she said. "The Kraang are going to poison the city's water supply with mutagen!"
April led the Turtles to the Kraang's warehouse.

Leonardo decided that Metalhead was too clumsy and noisy to help out. He ordered Metalhead and April to stay behind. The rest of the Turtles sneaked up on the Kraang.

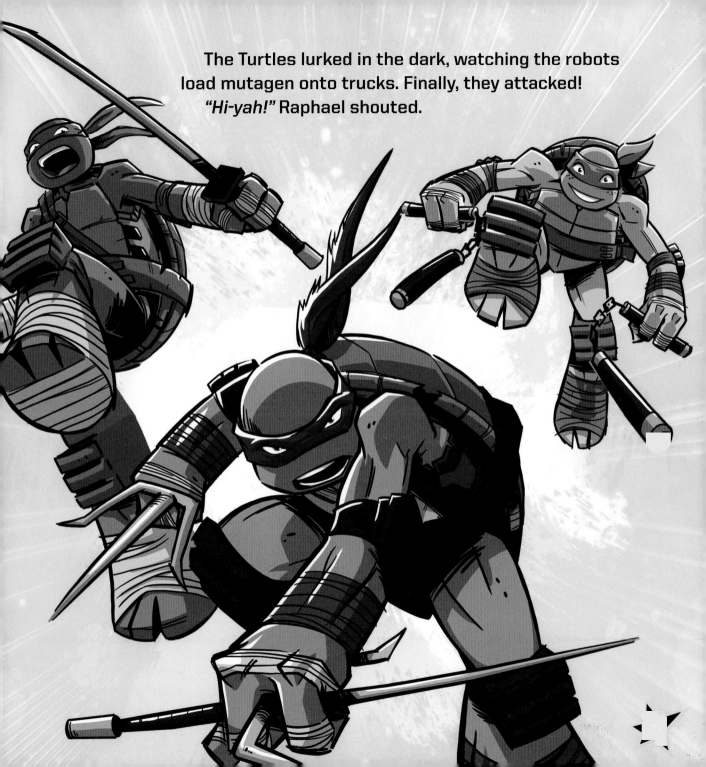

The Turtles lurked in the dark, watching the robots load mutagen onto trucks. Finally, they attacked! *"Hi-yah!"* Raphael shouted.

April and Metalhead were left on the rooftop. As they waited for the Turtles, an energy blast shot through the roof.

"They're everywhere!" Michelangelo shouted. "Run!"

It sounded like the three Turtles had been cornered by the Kraang.

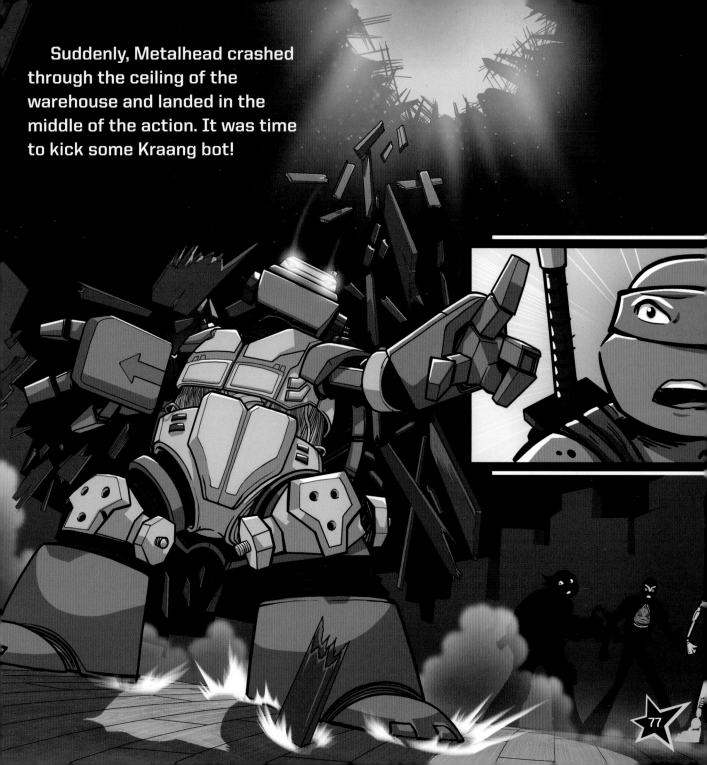

Suddenly, Metalhead crashed through the ceiling of the warehouse and landed in the middle of the action. It was time to kick some Kraang bot!

The battle with the Kraang continued. Metalhead really did seem invincible! The Kraang's lasers couldn't hurt him. The Turtles were finally winning!

Donatello watched from the lair, moving Metalhead with his controller. He blasted lasers all over the place. Finally, he found his target. *Boom!* The mutagen exploded.

But then, a Kraang blob jumped into Metalhead. Metalhead's eyes glowed red. Now the Kraang was controlling him! Evil Metalhead attacked the Turtles.

Donatello knew he had to save the Turtles from his own creation. He grabbed his *bo* staff and ran to the warehouse.

Donatello arrived just as Evil Metalhead was about to finish off the other Turtles. As the robot tried to blast him with a laser, Donatello jumped aside and the laser hit a huge beam. It came loose and fell on the robot!

Gears crunched and sparks crackled when Donatello stabbed his foe. Evil Metalhead was defeated once and for all! The Kraang brain jumped out and scurried away.

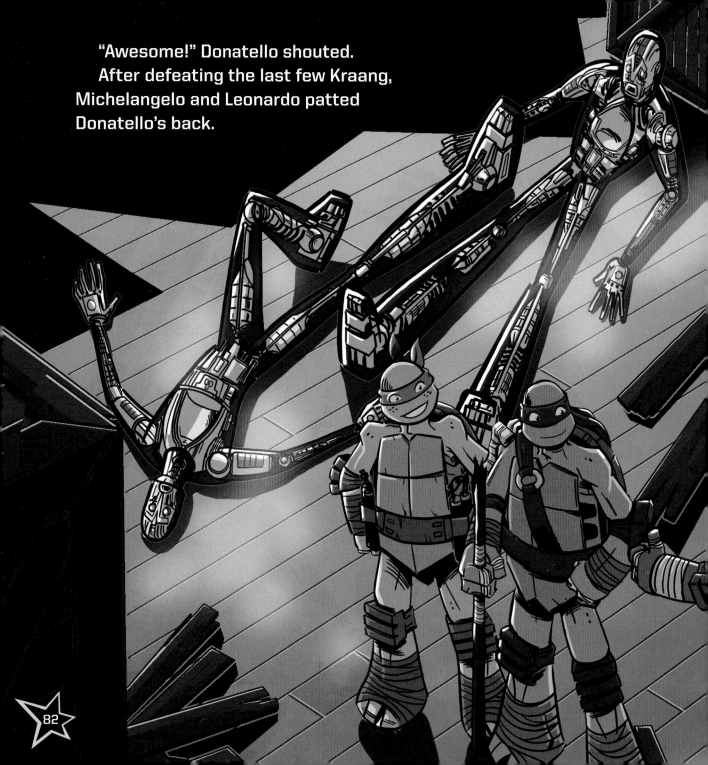

"Awesome!" Donatello shouted.
After defeating the last few Kraang,
Michelangelo and Leonardo patted
Donatello's back.

"Nice job, bro!" Michelangelo said.

Donatello was proud of himself.

"Not bad," Raphael said. "Except for the part where you got us into this mess in the first place."

Back in the lair, Donatello began to work on
a new project. Splinter thought he looked sad.
"What troubles you?" he asked.
"This was all my fault," Donatello said.
"Yes, you are responsible," Splinter replied.
"But you are also responsible for saving the city."

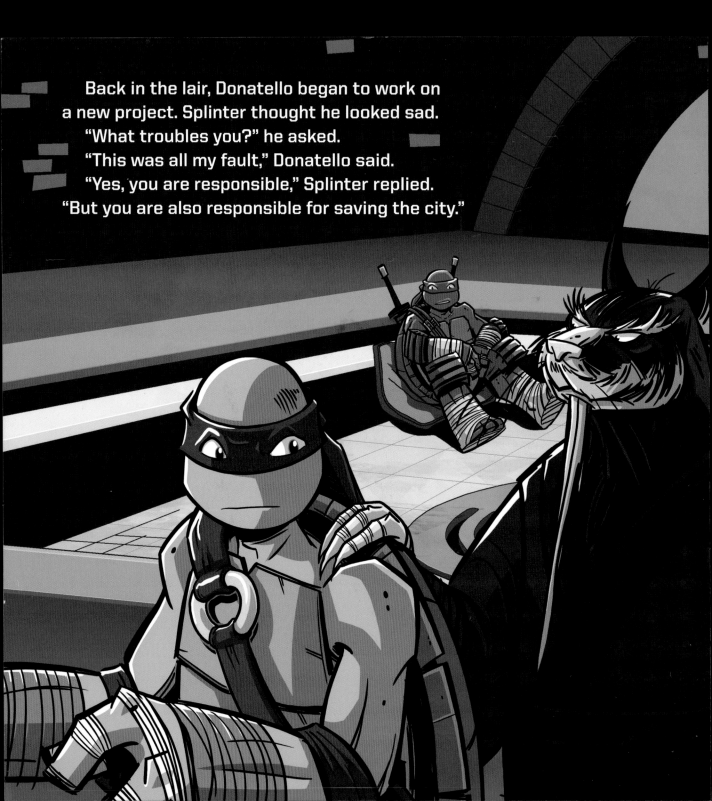